WATCHERS of the NIGHT

LINDA HOLZ

One

Minnesota to Iowa

The hallway was quiet except for the soft footfalls of the man who walked down its long dark length. He was tall, exactly six feet with a muscular build. Most women would find him quite handsome with his solid, broad powerful frame. His facial features were enhanced by perfect, sculptured cheekbones and a clean-shaven smooth chin. Topped with soft jet-black hair cut short to reveal an image most people knew him as, Mr. Clayton Cartel, a well-known physicist and chemist. For now, though, his features were masked as he walked the quiet hall of the building, he was so familiar with. Stopping in front of a door emitting a small shaft of light from under it he paused. Placing his hand on the knob he turned it slowly, then opened the door just enough to slip through and close it quietly behind him.

There was only one older man in the room with him now. The odor of ammonia and dimethyl sulfide mixed with the smell of animals kept in cages assailed his senses as he took in said cages containing several domestic house cats and one sedated leopard. Most of the room was in shadow, but he knew its contents well. Test tubes, Bunsen burners, and flasks were scattered on the counters lining the wall to his left. The wall he faced contained stainless worktables with sinks. Sealed wall cabinets were given space above the worktables. The wall to the right contained tables housing cages and one huge floor cage for the leopard. In the center of the room was a u-shaped desk containing several computers, a printer, a small lit lamp, papers scattered about with pencils, pens and small calculators. A small, two drawer file cabinet was pushed under one of the desks, close to where the old man sat, facing away from the door, and intent on his work. A half-eaten sandwich, a cold cup of coffee, and an empty bag of chips were sitting near his right elbow.

Cartel watched the old man writing intently in his notebook. He knew the man as Dave Matthews, having worked beside him on a number of occasions, tackling many a project. Tonight, though, was very different. Cartel did not appreciate being left out of this mysterious project Matthews was working on. He was angry that he was not allowed to participate.

Twenty minutes passed when Matthews finally laid his pencil down and picked up a syringe, which sat at his left elbow. Getting up he exited the U-shaped desk area and walked to a nearby counter. A number of test tubes were placed into a test tube holder. All were empty except one. Picking up the filled test tube he pushed the needle of the syringe through the cork until it reached the liquid inside. He filled the syringe. Walking back to his desk he turned off his lamp. Now the only light in the room was the moon, shining a pale-yellow glow throughout the room's interior, casting different shadows.

Grabbing his notebook, along with the syringe he strode to the door. He was taken completely by surprise when his right arm was grabbed and a sharp pain shot through his side. He gasped, trying vainly to hang onto the syringe so it would not crash to the floor into a million pieces. But in the end Cartel plucked it from his hand as Matthews weakened and fell to the floor.

Lying there Matthews was vaguely aware of the man as he strode to the desk to rummage through some papers. Not finding what he wanted he walked over to Matthews and promptly took the notebook. Then striding over to the test tubes, he plucked the half-filled tube from its resting place. All the while Matthews knew he was weakening fast. Reaching inside his coat pocket he brought out a small box. Looking above the door, with great effort he pressed a button on the box and saw a red-light flash, silently signaling help as he slumped forward landing on the box, his life's-blood ebbing slowing from the knife wound in his side.

Cartel was not aware of the red light flashing or the possibility of discovery until the faint tell-tale sign of a siren reached his ears. Swearing he quickly secured his loot as best he could and sped from the room, stepping quickly over Matthews, lying in the doorway.

Cathy Ryler sat quietly on the park bench, enjoying the peaceful night. Sounds of frogs mingled with the occasional cricket. In the distance the soft hoot of an owl could be heard. Stars sparkled in the sky, forming zodiac patterns if one looked close enough. A full moon smiled down at her. She would have loved to stay longer, but knew better because it was getting late and her sister would start to worry. She also did not want to be a potential victim as the town did have its side of those who would not blink twice when it came to causing someone harm.

The next day she would be leaving for home. It had been fun and she enjoyed visiting her sister, even though it was the first time she had been to Princeton, Minnesota. It was a nice town, although she missed her home in Manchester, Iowa and a part of her couldn't wait to be back there, where she felt safe and content, free to do what she wanted in her own world. Besides, Princeton was bit to large of a town for her.

Getting up she began to walk in the direction her sister lived. It wasn't very far, like three blocks, so she could take her time to enjoy the quietness of the night intermixed with an occasional car passing by. Two blocks later Cathy heard the first tell-tale sound of sirens. She stopped to listen. It was sad, in a way, that they had to disturb the quiet and peacefulness of the night, knowing that something had was happening, but then there was always the mystery; what had happened, who was hurt and why. Shaking her head she began walking again, and then stopped suddenly as she realized they were coming in her direction. She watched them as they passed, first, the ambulance, and then three police cruisers. 'Must be really serious,' she thought, 'to send so many police on the scene.'

She began walking again, hardly noticing that the sirens had stopped. Only the red lights flashed, mixing with blue, their reflections sweeping over bushes and trees, gliding across houses. She could tell without looking that they had stopped at the University of Research because it was only a block behind her.

The quietness returned and she began to relax once more. Unfortunately, it did not last long. She nearly jumped to the top of the highest tree when she heard the gun shots. She turned around, ready to take flight if necessary. Instead, she found herself on the ground, the breath nearly knocked from her, and a man on top of her. Stunned she gazed into the masked covered face of her assailant. The cold eyes of death stared back at her, hypnotizing. She could not bring herself to look away. Not until his eyes turned their attention elsewhere did her eyes lock on something on the side of his neck, her mind storing it there as she heard herself scream once, the sound piercing the air as her body began its struggle for freedom. She tried kicking him with her feet, attempted to twist him off with her hips, and push with her hands. She was pinned well and it was hard for her to fight, but she gave it her all. When she felt something sharp penetrate her right hip she screamed again, then sudden blackness overwhelmed her.

A few minutes passed when she woke to find an officer standing over her.

"Are you all right ma'am?"

"I think so. What happened?"

The officer reached down to help her to her feet and once there she felt herself weave slightly. It went unnoticed by the officer.

"We are looking for a murder suspect. My partner and I thought he went this way."

"Murder!?"

"Yes. How did you end up on the ground?"

She shook her head, trying to remember. "It happened so fast. One minute I am walking home, the next I'm lying on the ground. Something hit me hard."

"I understand. Why don't I escort you home and maybe you will be able to remember something on the way."

The highway stretched out before her as her car's tires skimmed its broad flat service. Cathy thought about that night, the police officer asking her questions to try and jog her memory, her sister worrying over her as well as her sister's friend and neighbor. She really tried to help the officer as best she could. They all felt it was the murderer who had knocked her down. She wanted to remember, but all she remembered was the pain, sharp pain that grew throughout the night from her right hip, but had stopped by morning. It was puzzling. She had not mentioned it to the officer, thinking it not necessary. She felt that she had bruised it somehow from the fall. What else could it be? So, she had kept her mouth closed and tried to think of a description of the man who they said had attacked her and killed a person.

But it was no use. Even now, as her car drove over the highway some ten miles from Waterloo, Iowa she still could not think of what the man looked like. She wished her memory would return. For now, she decided it was time to stop for a bite to eat. She felt a little light headed and her hip began to tingle as though it was asleep. When a turn off leading to a truck stop approached, she took it.

Parking the car, she got out and walked into the restaurant. Finding a seat, she waited for a waitress to take her order. She took note of the interior with its many tables and chairs, of people coming and going. Her mind began to wander to another day and time; when she sat at another truck stop near Iowa City. Across from her sat the man she loved and still loved, even though it had been over a year since he had died. She quickly wiped the tears from her eyes when she came out of her reverie and noticed the waitress standing beside her table. She smiled an apology and gave the lady her order, then watched her as she walked away. It was funny she thought, how just the smallest thing could bring the memory of her husband and her life with him come to the fore.

She winced when the tingling in her hip moved to her waist and quickly traveled down her right leg. She wished it would stop. What was wrong with her? As soon as she finished her meal, she would find a Casey's or 7-Eleven stores and purchase some Excedrin.

When her meal arrived the tingling had stopped, allowing her to enjoy her food. Tipping the waitress for bringing such a good meal she got up, paid the cashier and walked out of the building to her car. As she turned the key in the ignition the tingling began again. It spread rapidly from her hip to waist, right leg, continuing onto her left leg, her right arm and mid section. She waited, hoping it would soon pass as it had done in the restaurant. Maybe she should go see a doctor instead of buying pain killers? She shook her head in the negative as the tingled stopped. How would she explain it? —that she tingled all over! Besides, it wasn't too painful as it felt like a person's foot when it fell asleep. That could sometimes hurt, or be quite irritating, but this tingling was somewhat different. She began to drive, this time in search of a store.

It did not take her long when she found a 7-Eleven, sitting on the outskirts of town. Other places of business were nearby, a gas station, a car dealer, and a Pronto to name a few.

Upon entering the store, she decided it was time to use the bathroom. After asking where it was, she entered the small room, closing the door behind her. When her business was completed, she washed her hands, dried them, and then went to open the door. With her hand on the knob, she turned it, opening the door a crack, when the tingling began again. It spread rapidly and when it reached her head she could not move. She was on the floor by then, for her legs had given out on her. She could not stand. She was paralyzed, but she felt her body moving, shifting. God, how she wanted to scream, but couldn't. What was happening to her?

Her eyes could not focus well so she closed them. A moment passed and the tingling stopped. Slowly she opened her eyes to see if things were clear again. They were and she sighed with relief. She stood up to pick up her purse and leave. When she saw the countertop sink above her, and her purse sitting on the corner of it she just stared at it, frowning. Wasn't she standing up? Now that was a silly question. Of course she was standing.

Looking at the floor she gasped in shocked surprise. Her hands were no longer hands, but cat's paws. This is ridiculous she thought as she moved her left paw, then her right. Glancing to the side she saw a cat's body in every aspect, a domestic short hair to be exact, with dark fur. Her fur coat had a healthy luster to it as though she were very well taken care of, a pampered pet.

Sitting back on her haunches she began to think of her predicament. What was she to do? How was she to go home? She could not drive her car let alone picking up her purse and taking it to her vehicle. And where were her clothes? Then another terrible thought entered her mind: what if she never changed back! It was then that the voices reached her ears. Curious she went to the partially opened door and passed through. As she rounded a corner, she saw a man standing at the check out counter. A young woman stood on the other side, a look of shocked horror on her face. The man looked angry.

"Wake up lady, give me the money now! All of it or you're dead! Move it!" He moved the gun he held to emphasize his point.

The woman whimpered as she began to fumble with the register, her hands trembling uncontrollably. Silent tears ran down the side of her face.

"Come on bitch! Hurry up! I don't have all day!"

Cathy made up her mind. She had to get him away from that woman. Crouching low she walked behind the man, around the corner of the counter and down an isle. Reaching its end, she jumped onto a shelf and deliberately knocked something off, then quickly went to another isle.

"What was that? Is there someone else here? I thought this place was empty. I didn't sit in my car, watching all day for nothing."

Another thing fell to the floor.

"Who's there? Come out now or your dead."

Silence, nothing moved.

Looking at the woman he scowled at her. "You move and your history, lady!"

Walking slowly down an isle the man held his gun, ready to use at a second's notice. The woman watched him as though hypnotized with fear. She broke the trance when she felt something soft touch her hand. She was surprised to see a cat sitting on the counter, looking up at her. She watched as the cat moved to sit beside a returned VHS tape, which she had not had the time to put away. The cat looked at her again and set its paw on top of the tape. She glanced at the mirrors to see where the man was as he searched the isles, and then back again. The cat was gone. A moment later something else clattered to the floor.

The man looked at her to confirm her presence then turned back to his task. He was getting angry and frustrated.

The woman moved to where the tape sat. When she read the title, she was surprised by it and almost did not believe what she saw. The movie was called RUNAWAY staring Tom Selleck.

She couldn't believe it. The cat was telling her to run away. She was amazed by the whole thing. When she heard another item fall to the floor and the man swear and cuss she moved to action. Quickly pressing the alarm button, she ran for the door. Just as she ran through the man looked up and saw her. He swore and moved to take off after her. When she heard the faint sound of sirens, he thought it would be best to leave.

He got only a few feet from the counter, halfway to the door when he felt a sharp, piercing pain in his shoulder and neck. Yelling he instinctively reached around to remove it and touched soft fur. Turning his head slightly he saw the eyes of a cat. By then he was in agony, intense pain shooting through his body. This time, grabbing the cat by the scruff of its neck he tried pulling the feline off, but the teeth and claws only dug deeper, ripping flesh. The man screamed, rolling to the floor, trying to use any means to knock the cat off, bumping into shelves, the counter, rolling over and over, on the floor one moment, up the next. He didn't care about anything, but getting the cat off.

When Cathy saw the police run through the door, she quickly released him and left, dashing around the counter and back to the restroom, leaving the man on the floor moaning and groaning.

Reaching the small room, she sat down, looking at the partially open door and listened to the commotion in the other room. Even though she had taken a beating she worried more. Now what was she going to do? She couldn't stay here. How was she to get to her car, let alone carrying her purse? She could not leave it here. Releasing a long sigh, she continued to sit there and listen.

Glancing down at the floor she gasped. She looked at her hands, no longer paws. She blinked twice and got to her feet. There had been no tingling to let her know she was changing. Had she dreamed it all? It was possible that she had slipped and fell, hitting her head and, while she lay unconscious, had dreamed everything. The only problem with that idea was not feeling any pain or bump on her head. She decided to ignore it.

Collecting her purse, she walked out of the restroom and upon entering the main part of the store, realized it had not been a dream. Police were everywhere. A distraught cashier told her unbelievable story to an officer. Another placed hand-cuffs on the thief as he grimaced in pain; all the while mumbling to himself, "killer cat; killer cat!" Other officers rummaged through the isles looking for evidence and a possible stray cat as more walked around outside.

A part of her mind thought she could walk past them without being noticed, but it was not to happen. One of the officers walking the isles saw her and rushed over to barrette her with questions. Where was she during the hold-up? Did she hear anything, see anything? Did she see a cat in the store when she came in? The questions seemed to never end. An hour later, after leaving the officers her contact information, she was back on the road. Cathy quickly left the outskirts of Waterloo and Cedar Falls behind.

Two

Several days had passed finding Cathy sitting comfortably in her living room watching TV while she contemplated writing a quick shopping list for her trip tomorrow to Cedar Rapids. Grabbing her purse, which sat only inches from her she began searching its contents for an ink pen and piece of paper. As she dug into her purse, she felt the need to clean out her bag. Getting side tracked she reached for several fragments of paper and set them beside her on the couch. After finishing sorting out the odds and ends sitting in the bottom, such as some loose coins she replaced most of the items she had just taken out. When the small pile of papers was left, she began sorting them. Some were old receipts, which she quickly tossed into the wastebasket. A small calendar was in the assortment. She placed that back in her purse. Several pieces of blank paper followed the calendar, keeping one out for her list. Next was what looked like a grocery list in somebody else's handwriting stapled to a sheet with addition and subtraction problems on it. She frowned at these and threw them in the wastebasket. Now there was only one piece of paper left. She looked curiously at it. It was a sheet of typing paper folded twice, then one more time. She could tell there was something typed, which was odd. She did not even own a typewriter. Opening the paper, she looked at it and gasped. There were all kinds of figures on it. Chemistry was obviously involved. Some of the figures looked complicated. Some words she recognized from high school chemistry class, molecules and atoms. Some of the figures looked complicated. Where did such a paper come from? It looked like it might be a formula of some kind, the way it was listed on the paper. For the time being she would put it in a safe place until she figured out where it had come from.

Once that was done, she retrieved the piece of paper for her list. She had written down a few items when the type written formula entered her thoughts. She had always been fascinated with the figures used in chemistry, even though she did not understand them as to what they did. It would be kind of fun to make up her own kind of formula. On her list she wrote the word typewriter. Satisfied she sat back to peruse the contents of her list to make sure she had everything and noticed what was on the television screen. Turning it up, she stared at it in stunned silence. A show called 60 Minutes was featuring a subject on 'Weird and Unusual' happenings. One of the events shown at that moment revealed her in cat form coming to the aide of the cashier lady while the place was being robbed, only to disappear when the police arrived. Cathy blanched when she saw herself exit the restroom as the only witness who did not see anything. She had no idea she had been video taped. Turning off the TV she began to prepare for bed.

A few hours later Cathy began to toss and turn in her bed as she saw a man wearing a mask bump into her, knocking her off her feet. She struggled to be free, pushing with her hands. She felt the stabbing pain shoot through her hips. She screamed. Sweat beaded her forehead. Suddenly everything began to fade, but she still lay on the ground. It was when she started to sit up that she saw, coming out of the darkness, something walking toward her. She forced her eyes to focus in the hope of catching the details of the object.

Suddenly her eyes shot wide open, her mouth gaping as it began to form a scream. Her breathing was held back ready, at any moment to release a blood curdling, sharp, piercing cry as she watched a monstrous creature come toward her.

Its ears were in the shape of a big cat as they lay back against its head in a menacing gesture. The short tail swished back and forth rapidly. The animal's back arched as it sidled closer. The eyes were glaring yellow slits. The mouth was partially open to reveal several long fangs, dripping saliva and blood. There was no way the mouth could close properly because of the way they had grown. Even the paws of the beast were large. From each paw long talons reaching a good three inches or more scraped the ground with each step. Its fur was black, matted in places with dirt and blood. The mouth formed a snarl as it reached for her legs, touching one with its sharp fangs.

The scream that formed in her throat exploded loud and sharp into the room, echoing around her as she sat up in bed, sweat beading her forehead. She reached for her leg, rubbing the area that had been bitten. The leg hurt.

Catching her breath Cathy lay back on her sweat-covered bed. She lay there for what seemed like hours, but was really only a few minutes, willing herself not to close her eyes.

In Princeton Minnesota Cartel sat in a chair made of soft leather, a glass of expensive brandy in his right hand. He faced a large oak desk behind which sat another man who was in his mid fifty's. He was dressed in a black, very expensive, suede suit. He stared pensively at Cartel as he took a sip of the brandy, taking note of the black jeans and faded blue shirt. He had not shaved for a few days, seeing the results of a beard. He secretly hoped he did not have to deal with this man much longer.

"Did you find the woman you so conveniently ran into?"

"No. Not yet." Seeing the man's sudden discomfort Cartel added. "But we do have some leads."

"Like what?"

Now it was his turn to begin fidgeting, not because of being annoyed, but because of being nervous at being caught off guard.

"Well, we know that she was here visiting family and has left town."

When no more words came forth, he asked, "And where did she go?"

Cartel swallowed a few times before answering.

"I am not sure, but I am working on it. We already know her name is Cathy Ryler."

With those words the man lost his patience and shouted, "Well get off your ass and find her now! I want that formula you so carelessly gave her!"

Cartel stuttered, "B-but I h-had little choice. I-I didn't w-want the cops to grab me w-with the evidence. I p-put the notebook in a b-bush and went b-back later for it. I even had to get rid of the syringe and what was in it. I just threw it as far as I c-could."

"I don't care." Resting his hand on the notebook he continued, "The formula was folded up in this notebook that contains Matthew's scribbled notes. It fell out. I need you to get that formula no matter what!"

Those words were said with such finality that Cartel rose from his chair and quickly left the room. The other man sat for awhile in his chair behind the oak desk, thinking:

'How could he have hired such a bumbling oaf? Didn't he know the research lab would have an alarm system? He even worked at the place. He had planned everything so carefully. The money and research involved, the robbery and death of Mathews, and the syringe filled with all the dreams and glory of being rich, having something; if it worked, to offer other countries in the hope they could use it for warfare or whatever they liked. Now the syringe was gone and when the idiot went back later to look for it, he found it empty, a large crack in its side. If the contents of the syringe worked, he would have proof it worked, which would have given the formula credence. But now that was gone.'

A murderous rage overcame the man every time he thought of it every day there after. No matter what, he would get that formula, even if he had to kill to acquire it.

Clayton Cartel walked to his Audi A4 Sedan. Getting in behind the wheel he smiled to himself. He is such a foolish man. He had no idea. Cartel did not tell him the formula was accidentally given to the woman, this Cathy Ryler; since he thought all she had was the paper copy. Cartel never threw the syringe anywhere. He refilled it with the contents of the test tube and had it been right here with him in the car. He also knew where Miss Ryler went when she left town. Her little drama at a convenient store was shown on a news channel and then later on a 60 Minute documentary. Plus, he did not mind acting like an idiot to get what he needed. Now the only thing he had to do was get the copy of the formula he had slipped into her purse.

Cathy sat at her desk using her newly purchased typewriter, painstakingly retyping the list of chemicals on a clean sheet. She thought it would be easier and more fun to copy the original and make slight changes as she went, but she had no idea it would take so long. It had taken her several days to type only a fourth of it, while checking out books from the library to research the symbols. Now, two weeks later she was finishing up. Soon she was stashing the original in her bedroom. Her copy, she kept out to look at for awhile. When done she folded it; placing it with some papers by her typewriter. When she glanced at the clock, she noted that it was time to get ready for work. Forty-five minutes later she was on her way. The hours during her shift went by quickly, the day went well. When she punched out to end her shift, she was glad she had the next two days off.

A few minutes later found her walking up the steps to her apartment, thinking of things she wanted to get done before going to bed when she noticed her door was slightly ajar. It had been jimmied. A noise from inside caused her to freeze and listen. All her senses were alerted. She was only slightly aware of the tingling.

Pushing the door with her small body she walked through. Her cat eyes did a cautious search of her home. She did not go far when she saw a man standing in front of a book shelf, searching each book, and then tossing them to the floor. She quickly slid behind him and into her living room. Jumping on a chair she sat to watch. She studied him from head to toe. She noted how good looking he was with jet black hair cut short. What struck her the most was the birth mark on the back of his neck? Cathy had seen it before, but could not remember where.

When the man finished in the hallway he moved to the living room. He didn't pay any attention to her, so intent was he in his searching. He went through anything he could get his hands on, behind the couch, under cushions, moving furniture, rummaging through other bookshelves, littering the floor as he went. Seeing her waste basket, he looked inside, taking out the stapled sheets she had thrown away. When he came to her desk where her typewriter sat, he started with the drawers, dumping their contents and scattering them as he searched. Finishing that, he began leafing through the pages sitting on top. Her ears flicked forward and back with the exclamation of joy at finding what he was looking for. She jumped to the desk to see what it was. She only got a glimpse of it before he folded it and stuffed it into his shirt pocket. Without thinking he patted her on top of her head and walked out the door. She quickly jumped down to follow. She had no trouble slipping through the door as he passed through, but almost got her tail clipped when she jumped into the car.

The man did not notice her as she settled into the back seat to wait. It wasn't a very long wait because he drove only a couple of blocks to where a phone booth was. She quickly followed him out the door as he got out. She sat down next to his leg as he dug into his pocket for a quarter, then dialed a number.

Soon he was talking avidly to someone on the other end. Certain words reached her small ears, taking the information in eagerly.

"Yeah, I found it…no she was not home, just the cat. Be over in a bit to deliver."

The man hung the handset onto the phone's hook and walked around the car to get in. Immediately Cathy jumped to follow and when the car door opened, she leaped to the floor of the car and crawled under the seat. As she squirmed her way to the other side, she heard the man exclaim," What the…!" Jumping onto the back seat hands suddenly grasped her middle she found herself going over the top of the front seat and back outside.

"You can't be in here?" Come on, out of the car. You can't come with me. Here now," as he tossed her on the curb of the sidewalk, "go back where you came from." Before she had a chance to react, he shut the car door, with him inside and her out.

She sat down, her tail switching in agitation as she watched the car stop at the intersection, and then turn north. This was not her day. Well, she might as well go home and clean up the mess the man had made during his search.

She blinked when the ground suddenly receded from her and she felt hands grasping her around the middle. Looking around she saw a toddler's chubby little face grinning happily at her. He turned with her to face his mother who stood in the door of the gas station.

"Ma-ma…found a kee-kee…kee-kee!"

"Yes, I see. You need to put the kitty down so we can go inside and pay our bill."

"Kee-kee ma-ma, kee-kee comes with." The child began to follow his mom on stout chubby legs as she disappeared inside through the automatic door.

'Great,' Cathy thought, 'this is really not my day.' Her tail switched rapidly, becoming more agitated. "Would you let me go please?"

When she suddenly landed on all fours on the pavement, she shook her head and looked to the child, who ran as fast as his small legs would carry him to his mother as she exited the station to find him.

"Ma-ma, kee-kee tawk! Kee-kee tawk ma-ma!"

What?! Cathy blinked, taken aback at the words. She didn't talk out loud, did she? But how could she, she was a cat, unless that part of her stayed the same when she was changed. If that was so, then she was going to have to be a bit more careful from now on.

The mother picked up her child. "Yes dear, I know. Kitty went meow, meow. Let's get some ice-cream then go home."

Cathy sat by the gas pumps for a minute or two after the car carrying the child and his mother drove away that she also decided to go home.

Clayton Cartel drove into Princeton, Minnesota after over four and a half hours of driving. He was impatient to get this done. Parking his car in front of the place where the man who hired him lived, he paused briefly to look at the typed paper of the formula. Hopefully this would appease the man and he would get the money owed to him. After that he would find out what this formula was all about, including the contents of the needle. Leaving his car, he walked to the door and knocked. The door soon opened by the butler, a robust little man in his early fifties.

"Mr. Fabian is in the den."

"Thank you," answered Cartel.

Walking down a hall, lined with occasional framed pictures, potted plants and chairs, he turned into the first room on his left. Fabian sat in a soft chair looking into the fireplace. A glass of wine sat on the coffee table.

"About time you got here." Fabian turned to look at Cartel, "what kept you?"

Cartel frowned. Didn't he know the long drive to get here? "Traffic wasn't good."

Fabian snorted. "Let's see the formula."

Cartel handed him the piece of paper. Fabian perused its contents, and then smiled. Folding the paper, he put it on the coffee table, and then reached inside his coat pocket. Instead of an envelope containing money his hand held a gun.

Cartel looked at the weapon, then Fabian, no longer smiling.

"I suppose you're not going to tell me what that formula is about?"

"Afraid not, you know too much as it is. You worked in the same building as Matthews so you should have some idea of what he was working on."

Not saying anything Cartel shook his hand slightly, releasing the knife from his sleeve into his palm. The moment it touched his hand he swung it out and forward, releasing the knife as the bullet hit him in the chest, knocking him back to land on the floor. He lay there stunned for a moment, and then he did not move.

Fabian walked over to him just as the butler entered the room. The butler looked at the man on the floor, and then at Fabian.

"You are hurt sir. Do you need help?"

"No, I am fine Simon. It is just a shoulder wound. We need to get rid of the body. That's more important right now."

"Of course, sir, no problem."

Getting a blanket Simon rolled Cartel onto it then rolled the blanket around him. Fabian watched as his butler picked up the bundle, secretly admiring the man's strength, his robust nature. Walking to the garage Simon placed the body in the trunk and drove away.

A few miles out of town he turned onto a gravel road. Traveling a way, he found what he was looking for, a deep overgrown ravine. Placing the blanket parallel with the ravine he grabbed the end. Hanging on he pushed, allowing the blanket to unwind, releasing its heavy burden into the earth's cavity.

Turning Simon walked back to the car, placed the blanket in the back seat and drove away. He never noticed the blanket had moved several times and by the time it hit the bottom of the ravine Cartel was fully awake. His body ached. He felt his chest, found the slug and pulled it from the bullet proof vest. Moving to sit up he felt another stabbing pain in his upper leg. Reaching into his pants pocket he brought out the cap covering the needle of the syringe, cracked and broken. Reaching in again Cartel brought out the syringe, now empty. Angry he threw it, and then rubbed the area the needle had penetrated.

Having had enough of his surroundings, Cartel began to climb out. By the time he reached the top he was filled with rage. Pulling off his shirt and vest he began to walk, and then run as the drug moved through his system.

Three

After Cathy came home, cleaned up the mess she decided on a nap. Settling on the couch she turned the TV on and soon fell asleep.

The yellow cat ran around houses and across streets. He raced to a building in time to see another cat enter. Following her inside he sat in the doorway watching her as she sat on a table and a man who wore cowboy boots, a well-worn pair by the look of them. He wore tacky black jeans and a faded denim shirt. His hands were not large like some men, the fingers skinny and long. There was dirt under some of his fingernails while the others were chewed to nothing. He obviously had a nervous habit. His being thin did not compliment him at all, his clothes hanging loosely on his body. He was not a handsome man. His face was well worn denoting his age to be over forty-five. Bags under his eyes told of lack of sleep. The beginnings of a beard outlined his face and lines on his forehead said that he frowned a lot, of which he was doing now as he searched her home. His hair was cut short revealing something on his neck. Her eyes glued to it as memories flooded back to her, falling heavily to the ground, struggling under a heavy weight for freedom. A sharp stabbing pain in her hip as the needle penetrated her skin. Even though it was partially hidden it stood out in stark detail before her eyes, a birthmark in the shape of a capital C.

Cathy sat straight up, breathing heavily. She remembered now where she had seen that birthmark. On the neck of the man who searched her home. He was the same one who killed that scientist and knocked her down, injecting her with something that allowed her to shape shift. But why would he want her list she had worked so hard on. She thought for awhile, taking the time to really think. Then it dawned on her. He was after the original one that was hidden in her bedroom and took hers by mistake. But what was it about? To think more on it she decided to go for a walk.

Two young teenagers pushed the door to the tavern open, laughing when the door banged against the building. They both tried to balance themselves as they staggered to their car. One of them searched in his pants pocket for the keys. Once found he unlocked the car and they both climbed in. Inserting the key in the ignition he turned it. Hearing the sound of the engine he put it in gear and drove away. Neither one noticed the person who ran out of the tavern to stop them from driving. When he realized he was too late he cursed vehemently, wishing he could go after them. It was his car they were driving. He prayed that his son David and his friend Roy would be alright and rushed back inside to make a phone call. He could get into real trouble if they were busted, got hurt, or hurt someone else. They promised not to leave until he was ready to take them home. He should have known better. He should have hidden the keys.

Roy whistled loudly out the window at some girls walking on the sidewalk and laughed when they stuck their noses in the air and disappeared into a nearby house. He was knocked back into the car when it suddenly swerved and hit some garbage cans, scattering them, then over to the other side, running up onto the curb.

"David, slow down. You might hit something." He laughed at his joke, as David responded with a loud belch.

They turned onto another side street, bumping into a parked car before taking off again. It was then they could make out a shape of something in the road.

"David, be careful, don't hit it!"

"Oh, why not, it's only a cat."

The car shifted into high gear, taking on speed.

"Noo…don't…David!!"

As the car came toward Cathy she looked into the headlights, then jumped straight in the air as the car passed under her. She heard the tires screech to a halt. When the boys excited, they ran back to see a cat standing in the road.

"Where did the woman go? I swear I saw a woman. Did you see her eyes? They glowed just before she jumped," queried Roy.

"Are you crazy? I told you it was just a cat. I think you had too many beers tonight. David shook his head at his friend and went back to the car.

Roy frowned, looking at the cat as it walked to the curb to disappear into the bushes. Turning around Cathy sat within the bushes watching Roy stand there for a moment, shake his head, and then walk to the car to leave with his friend. That was close. And her eyes glowed!? Like a cat she thought, sarcastically. Was she eventually to always be a cat? Sighing she decided it was time to go home.

Four

A week later Sergeant Derek Ryan looked at the mutilated and almost unrecognizable body as it lay partially concealed in some bushes. This was not the way he wanted to start the day, but start it he did. In all of his ten years of being a policeman and one year being a sergeant, he had never seen anything as horrid and gut-wrenching as this. Other officers immediately began to sanction off the area to keep people out. The ME arrived shortly after, made a quick assessment to finish with a more detailed autopsy later, at the morgue. The coroner arrived while the ME was still there and winced noticeably at the condition of the body before beginning his work. The ME was an old pro at this, seeing all kinds of distorted limbs and body parts during his profession, so the coroner's response was a bit surprising to him.

People stretched their necks high above others as they tried to get a look at the body, officers keeping the over-eager at bay. All of this went unnoticed by Ryan as he went through the normal routine of asking questions and looking for evidence, as well as any witnesses. A few other officers would be doing the same. As for the scene, it was the same as when he checked out the two bodies that were found only a couple of days ago. The ground was torn up around the bodies. Only a small portion of the body had been consumed, the rest chewed and ripped to pieces. It was as though the creature, whatever it was, was mocking them, telling them that he did not have to kill for food, but whenever he wanted to, and no one could stop him. A chill went through Ryan's body at the thought.

The reason he said a creature was because of the prints that were found around and near the body. They were the prints of a big cat, but larger, too large even for a tiger. Pictures and several plater molds were taken.

Now he had the task of trying not to let the townspeople panic and the news media's arrival on the scene would not help matters, and again he wished he could have started the day differently.

Several hours later Derek sat in his recliner with his remote control in one hand and can of beer in the other. He had skipped supper, his stomach suddenly revolting at the last moment with even the thought of eating. Usually he always ate regularly, three meals a day and an occasional snack. He never overate and so never gained or lost much weight. And it helped to work out in the gymnasium. He was healthy and strong, his years on the force helped him to maintain his physical condition. There were days when his job did not allow him to get to the gymnasium. And this had been one of them. He could not believe he was actually sitting down. It had been hours since he had last sat, which had been a quick bite at dinner time. Now with a good movie and a cold can of beer he felt relaxed.

It was in this relaxed state that a strange sound reached his ears, even over the sound of the movie. He moved slightly so he could figure out its direction, if it was repeated. It did not take long for that to happen. The sound was repeated again from the direction of the kitchen. He rose slowly from the recliner as his hand reached for his gun sitting on the coffee table, ready to use it if necessary. He held the weapon in front of him when the sound became continuous.

Flipping the light switch on in the hope of startling the person he entered the room, gun aimed straight ahead as his eyes quickly scanned the interior. He relaxed, shook his head and smiled when a pair of eyes looked at him briefly before returning back to the empty can of tuna that Derek had forgotten to throw away. He forgot to close the window again. This yellow feline friend had visited a few times before, but the last time was the final straw. The animal had made off with a whole trout which had taken him a whole afternoon to catch.

Derek picked the cat up and placed him on the window sill and was about to give him a gentle shove out when the animal suddenly stiffened. It's back arched, the tail doubling in size as the fur rose to spread across its back, making the animal look twice its size. The cat growled from deep within, hissing and spitting wildly before turning back to run through the kitchen and disappear into the rest of the house.

"What the hell got into you!? Hey wait, you can't go in there. Come back here!" Derek quickly followed to try and find the elusive creature. So, he wasn't there to hear the rustling noise outside or to see the huge face of a killer peer in his window.

The next morning Derek sat at his desk in his office going over the notes and reports of both cases. The main thing he saw was trying to identify the footprint of the animal. Finally, he came to the conclusion that he should go to the local library with a picture of the print. They might be able to help him. He also had to arrange a curfew. The attacks happened after dark. Setting the curfew before then would curtail any more attacks, or backlash having the creature find a different means of attack. Either way he had to try.

He jumped when his phone rang. He quickly picked up the receiver, not giving it a chance to ring again.

"Hello, Sergeant Derek Ryan here. How can I help you?"

"Yes. Good morning, Sergeant Ryan. My name is Patrick Blake from the county morgue. I have the results of the autopsy on the latest victim. If you have time, I can run you through what we got."

"No problem. I can be there in about twenty minutes."

"Sounds good," then he hung up.

Finishing his cup of coffee Derek left his office. He was not looking forward to visiting the morgue. No matter how clean the place was there was always a certain smell left behind and he always smelled it. A few minutes later he was walking up to the basement of the hospital, the lowest part of the building. To his left was the loading dock area, so funeral homes could pick up the deceased.

Approaching the door, he opened a gray box on the wall to his left and took out the receiver. Announcing himself he hung the phone up and waited. Soon a security guard opened the door and he was inside.

Walking a short way Derek noticed a small, but neat office to his left. To the right of the office were the coolers where bodies were stored. The rest of the room contained the autopsy suite, where examinations were performed. Near the center he saw the autopsy table. Beside the table stood Dr. Blake dressed in a white, blood-stained gown that covered his black jeans and red shirt, a mask covering his nose and mouth and surgical gloves for his hands. Derek watched him place an organ onto a nearby scale to get its weight. Once recorded on a blackboard Blake turned to face Derek. Walking over the tiled floor and passing several sinks Derek walked up to the table that contained the remains of the latest victim.

"I hope you know you have one heck of a killer on your hands. This is the third body in less than a week? Same killer, for sure! The time of death was four in the morning. The cause of death was the precise placement of teeth placed over the neck of the victim and driven into the flesh," Blake pointed to parts of the body above the shoulder. "From that point the animal ripped her head almost clean off. Death was instantaneous. After that he went to down, continually driving its long teeth deep into her flesh. This is where the puzzle comes in. The teeth are triple the length of a tiger. The only animal I can think of being closely related is a saber tooth tiger, and they have been extinct for millions of years."

Derek's gaze quickly moved from the body and looked at the doctor as though he were crazy. "That's impossible. How…?"

"I don't know how, but you sure have your work cut out for you."

Derek had seen enough. Stunned he left the doctor to his work, deciding it was time to visit the local library. Once settled into a booth with several selected books in front of him he set to work. Finding pictures of paw prints he checked the measurements with his sample. It was huge in comparison to the saber tooth and did not match any other big cat. Finally, he settled on a description of the saber tooth tiger: strong neck muscles were used to sink long teeth deep into flesh.

They would subdue their prey with their forelimbs, holding them down. Having weak jaws, they would drive the teeth into the prey using their neck muscles, not chomping down. Saber tooth tigers were most likely ambush hunters, with strong limbs and necks. Realizing the late time Derek decided to call it a day and as he drove home the words echoed through his head.

Five

Cathy left her house as darkness began its battle with the sun and as always happens at this time the sun loses its battle to fight again in the morning. This was her favorite time of the day and she always enjoyed taking a walk, but not for this night, because tonight she would be hunting; hunting for a killer. After hearing about the creature, as the media was calling it, Cathy knew she needed to find it and kill it.

She began by walking around her block, and then spreading out to include another block and another until she ended up at the park. There were a few people out but none that gave her an inkling of the danger. As she walked through the park, she noticed a yellow tomcat as it walked across the open area intent on reaching the shaded woods on the East Side of the park.

Her attention shifted momentarily to note a couple walking hand in hand as they entered their car and left the park. It was then that the tingling began and the danger was near. She was glad she stood in the lengthening shadow of a tree so no one could see her shape shift. She quickly scanned the area for the danger, grateful for the darkness to help conceal her dark shape. She could not see any danger as her gaze swept the park, her feline eyes stopping when she saw the yellow Tom. The animal stopped abruptly, staring straight at where it would have disappeared if and had continued its journey. Ears flat against its head, back arched making it resemble a small camel, all of its hair stood straight in the air as he began to hiss and spit at something as it emerged from the trees. It was then that the danger appeared. In vivid, stark detail her nightmare stood before her. It closely resembled a saber tooth tiger or Smilodon but there were things that made it different and not related in any way to the big cat. She was particularly fond of the prehistoric beasts and had done some research on a few, the saber tooth tiger being one. Although being no longer than a modern tiger of which could be ten feet long, four feet high and weigh over sixty pounds. It had a deeper body, and thicker legs and almost no tail. This one had a long tail, but like a saber tooth its shoulders and loins bulged with muscles, the huge paws and retractable claws three or four inches long.

The head was a big difference. There were no saber-like teeth curving down from the upper jaw. Instead, several long fangs protruded from the upper and lower jaws to mingle with smaller ones. The mouth could not close properly because of the way they were proportioned.

The animal also resembled a beast called Thylacosmilus (pouched chisel). A marsupial closely related to the kangaroos than the cats. It walked on four paws and was able to hunt big, thick-skinned animals and its stabbing teeth developed to enable it to kill in the same way as the Saber-tooth.

She was jolted from her reverie when the creature suddenly leaped the short distance, pinning the cat to the ground. It struggled under the huge paw, trying to free itself, straining with the effort to inflict some kind of pain in return. To Cathy it looked as though the creature had just caught a mouse. As the jaws moved closer to the yellow tom, its fangs, only inches away, she could no longer remain silent.

"Let—him—go!"

The creature stopped his assault to look for the source of the voice. Who dared to approach him? The darkness moved slightly as he swept the park with his gaze, noticing trees, bushes, park benches and the odd shape below one tree. His eyes focused as the shape of the Black Panther took form then widened slightly as he made contact with a pair of yellow cat eyes, panther eyes.

Cathy, on the other hand, knew that she dared not look away because if she did, he would go for her throat in an instant. The creature moved to face this Black Panther so as to assess the strength and weaknesses of this new enemy, releasing the Yellow Tom cat who took quick advantage of its freedom running for cover. Cathy stood her ground trying hard not to show any fear. This thing was a killer. It deliberately cut down its victims', slaying them without mercy. As it began to step toward her, she involuntarily moved back a foot.

The creature's mouth fell open as though grinning. It sensed fear. He loved fear. In his victim's it meant victory for him. A weakness he could easily feel. He moved toward her in the hope that her fear would overwhelm her. Cathy did feel fear, but as she watched the creature come at her she felt the need to protect herself, to survive.

Derek Ryan left his small house that he had rented. Getting into his car he turned the ignition to start the engine and quickly drove off. He thought it would be nice to go to the all-night video rental to find a good movie to watch. He was bored and not in the least bit tired. Nobody was in the store to give him any competition for movies so he picked out a couple. In no time at all he was back in his car and headed back toward home.

As he drove, he decided to get another six-pack of beer and something to munch on so he turned down another street, deciding on a short cut to the nearest Casey's. He passed several houses on either side. The road curved suddenly to the right bringing him face to face with a park, one of several in the town.

His headlight beams sliced through the darkness ahead of him, and as he began the turn, they brought out in stark detail the two forms locked in combat. His eyes widened as he braked the car to turn it to the side of the street and park, bumping the curb.

He checked his .34 Magnum, making sure it was loaded and leaving his car he quickly and cautiously made his way to the two fighters. With them in full view, his gun trained on them he took in the situation. He recognized the one from the description that he imagined the creature to be. He was the one killing people. The other he did not recognize right away and when he did, he realized it was a black panther. The animal was not doing well because at that moment the creature sunk its fangs deep in the shoulder and neck area, making the panther cry out and jolting Derek into firing his weapon. Unfortunately, it only grazed the beast's shoulder making him release the Panther, letting her collapse to the ground and directing his gaze in Derek's direction. Derek was momentarily taken aback as he stared at the fangs and dripping blood and the upper lip curving up in a sneer. When it spoke, he took an involuntary step backward.

"You-will-die-for-this!" the words were run together as one, as spittle and blood issued forth from each syllable. The creature was angry that he had been cheated out of his prey, not to mention his one main enemy in life. But he also knew what a gun could do as he took quick advantage of the man's astonishment and immediately fled.

Derek recovered quickly as he saw the creature flee and fired a few shots at the receding figure, missing miserably. It moved with lightening speed. He watched for a moment longer, his weapon trained on the area where it had disappeared making sure it would not return before he pivoted around to look at what lay at his feet.

The animal was unconscious. He noticed the cuts and scratches marking the sleek black coat, the worst being the wound on its shoulder. Derek bent down to examine the huge feline more closely, wondering if the cat was alive or not when he saw her eyes open.

"Please...leave."

He was stunned to hear her speak but quickly pushed it aside.

"No, you need help."

"No...doctors, please go. I will be...all right."

She began to struggle, attempting to rise so as to enforce her theory but only fell back to the ground again. "Please go...before..." The cat's eyes closed and it lay still.

Before what, Derek thought. Before that creature came back? His puzzled frown quickly disappeared as his eyes widened, his mouth fell open in astonishment. Unconsciously moving backward, a step but never letting his eyes leave the cat, he watched as the animal moved and changed form into that of a woman, a beautiful woman. He also noted that the cuts and gashes had disappeared from the naked form as he gazed in wonder and shock at the shapely curve of her thighs, hips and breasts. He was jolted back to reality as he saw blood flowing through the valley of those breasts. The wound on the shoulder had not completely healed. It was too deep.

He quickly stripped off his jacket and covered her with it the best he could and picking her up he took her to the car and from there to his home, totally missing her cloths lying under her. He was sure he could treat her wound himself and not have to take her to a hospital since it had partially healed somewhat in the transformation. Derek understood now why she insisted on no doctors. What he had witnessed was amazing and totally unbelievable. Questions rolled through his mind and when he laid her in his bed, he saw her wound had started to bleed again. He quickly dressed it and sat back in a soft plush chair that resided beside the bed. He watched her as she breathed, noting the soft lines of her face. The last he remembered as his eyes closed was the darkness of her hair as it lay in soft rivulets around her face and over the blankets.

The sun's rays broke into the quiet room, filtering through and around the mini blinds. As the rays reached out, they chased the darkness and shadows away, their tendrils touching the floor, walls and furniture, trying to stretch as far as the mini blinds would allow, causing Derek to squint his eyes as one reached across his face. The rays were persistent, getting stronger and brighter with time, forcing Derek to move and blink his eyes open.

At first, he was disoriented until his eyes rested on the woman lying on his bed. Then everything from last night came flooding back. He watched her then, studying her as she slept. For a moment, which seemed to stretch into infinity, he sat in silence until he noticed that her eyes were open and she was looking at him. Immediately Derek came to attention. Rising from the chair he was beside the bed in two strides. He placed a hand on her forehead.

"How are you doing?" he asked.

"Okay, if I forget that I feel a little stiff and sore, plus my shoulder hurts like crazy and a splitting headache." She wished she could remember what happened.

"I'm not surprised. That bite was so deep that it still took stitches even though some had healed during your shape shifting. Are you hungry?"

"Yes, a little."

"Good. I will see what I can rustle up."

After he left Cathy scanned the room for her clothes. When she first woke up and realized that she had nothing on under the covers she almost panicked, refusing to think that a strange man whom she had never met before had undressed her.

Now her only thought was to get out. She could not see where her clothes were from her position so she tried to sit up to scan the rest of the room and felt a shooting stab of pain lightening bolt through her shoulder, making her fall back against the bed. She closed her eyes from the burning sensation, waiting for it to pass. When it did a thought struck her as she recalled the exact words he said before he left the room. She now remembered last night, especially the man as he stood over her and had witnessed her change. Plus, her clothes were somewhere in the park. Why they did not transfer onto her body after the change, she did not know, a fluke, perhaps.

Accepting defeat for now she lay there staring at the ceiling, trying to come up with a solution, not realizing that her eyes, after awhile, had closed. Five minutes later Derek entered the room, and seeing that she was asleep, quietly left the way he had come.

Cathy slept most of the day to awaken sometime after the supper hour. The room was dark and she was alone. To add to things she was very hungry, having not eaten in almost twenty-four hours. Maybe if she moved slower this time, she would be able to at least find the kitchen. Since she could not find something to wear, she decided to wrap one of the blankets around her. She made it to her feet all right, but once there she closed her eyes as a wave of dizziness swept through her head and she felt herself teetering. Cathy barely felt two strong arms encircle her to prevent her from falling to the floor, and then lift her back to the bed.

When she felt the soft warm covers surround her again her head began to clear and her eyes opened. She saw the man leaning over her with his hand near her face. Had he been slapping her face to awaken her?

"Well, hello again. May I ask what you were trying to do?"

"I was hungry," she mumbled.

"Well, you need not have worried. I was bringing a tray in when I saw you getting out of bed. You don't have all your strength back yet. Be patient."

Cathy watched him as he got off the bed, propped her up with pillows and walked over to a small table where the tray sat. She lost all interest in him as the tray was set in front of her and the aroma from the plates reached her.

For awhile Derek did not say anything as he watched her eat. It was good to see her have such an appetite.

When she took her last bite of food and a long drink of milk, he thought now was the time to talk.

"Do you feel up to talking now?"

She gave him a sideways glance as she sat her glass on the tray.

"I guess it is about time. I'll try to answer any questions you have." With that she settled against the pillows and waited as Derek removed the tray and set back in his chair.

"Well, maybe we could start with introductions. My name is Derek, Derek Ryan."

"I'm Cathy Ryler."

"Cathy. That's a…nice name." He was going say fitting, because the first three letters spelled cat, but decided not to. "Has anyone ever called you 'cat' for short?"

Cathy smiled as she remembered fondly how her father had called her cat when she was a child. He was dead now and she missed him dearly.

"Yes, my father. When I was between the ages of two and eight, he would call me his 'little kitty-cat'. He died shortly after my ninth birthday."

"I'm sorry."

"It's all right. I suppose you want to know why I change and what started it all?"

Derek didn't answer, waiting for her to continue and she did. What she said was amazing and startling. His mouth fell open a number of times in shock disbelief as he tried to sort it all out.

"You mean to tell me that if you sensed danger of any kind you would change?"

"Yes, it seems to be the only time unless there is something I have not discovered yet. I only just found out that I can talk like I am now and still be the panther." She did not tell him of the ability to transform into a house cat as well.

"The man who injected you with this strange formula, they have not found him yet?"

"No and it was later discovered by the police that he had killed a scientist to steal this formula just minutes before he ran into me."

"This is unreal!"

Cathy nodded her head as she released a big yawn as her eyes closed, to open again in a sleepy fashion. When Derek saw this, he suddenly regretted his curiosity. She needed her rest, not a question-and-answer session.

"I'm sorry, I should not have been keeping you awake this long." Reaching over he took the empty tray from the small table and walked to the door. "You get some sleep now." He turned and left, closing the door behind him.

Cathy lay there in silence for a moment going over the conversation in her mind, while at the same time wondering if she could trust this man. As her eyes drifted shut, she felt that she could.

An hour later Derek sat in the soft comfortable chair beside the bed and slept for a few hours. It was during that time that a sound reached his sub-conscious, alerting him to the fact that something was not right. He sat still for a moment, eyes closed and listening. When the sound was repeated, he opened his eyes. It was directly in front of him. His attention turned to the bed and the occupant ensconced there. He jumped to his feet and went to the bed. Cathy's head moved from side-to-side and she moaned again as Derek put his hand to her forehead, even though it wasn't necessary. Derek could tell just by looking at her that she was burning up. What had happened? Damn, she had been doing well, now this fever. Somehow, he had to bring it down, and fast. He thought for a moment. There was one way and he prayed that it would work. He quickly stripped the clothes from his body and slipped beneath the covers. His legs slid down next to hers. One arm went over the flatness of her stomach to reach his other arm, which had slipped underneath to bring her close up against his chest. He tried to cover her as much as he could with his own body while at the same time trying to forget the softness of her skin and scented fragrance of her hair. He noted the silken strands as they lay across his shoulders. He forced himself to lay his head beside hers and close his eyes. Her frantic movements soon stopped and her breathing was normal, but all this went un-noticed to Derek as he, to fell into a deep slumber.

That morning only a few clouds floated across the sky as the sun once more appeared on the horizon. The angry chatter of a squirrel brought Derek's eyes open to focus on the ceiling, bringing him out of the beautiful dream he was having. When he looked down, he realized it was not just a dream. Cathy still lay in his arms. Her eyes were closed in peaceful slumber. He carefully brought one hand up to feel her forehead. The fever had broken. It had worked. Quietly he disentangled himself so as not to disturb her and sat on the edge of the bed. He almost jumped straight up to a standing position when he heard her voice.

"What do you think you were doing?"

Derek felt himself blushing slightly, suddenly feeling embarrassed. Like the kid caught with his hand in the cookie jar. He thought it best not to turn around to face her. The words seemed to stick in his throat, but forced them out.

"I'm sorry. You had a fever and you were moaning and tossing around."

Reaching for his pants, which lay on the floor nearby he quickly slipped them on, standing to zip them.

"I didn't know what else to do in order to break your fever. It was the only thing I could think of. I'll go make some breakfast."

With that he strode to the door and left, leaving Cathy with a very vivid memory of his passing. A few minutes later he returned, carrying a tray. The aroma of scrambled eggs, sausage and toast filled her nostrils and she suddenly realized how hungry she was. Adjusting the tray on her lap as he handed it to her, she mumbled a thank you and started eating. She realized she had developed a quick attack of shyness as she remembered the feel of his arms as they encircled her and the full length of his body close to hers. She was grateful for the distraction of the food so she didn't have to think of anything more to say.

"Will you be all right for a couple of hours? I really should check in at the station. My department is probably wondering what happened to me since I am usually there by now."

"Yes, I'll be fine. Go ahead." Good, she thought, if he left for awhile, it would give her a chance to get her bearings and make a decision to stay or leave.

Derek, on the other hand felt the need for some space. He had to do some serious thinking and he could not do it here. He didn't like lying either, because he knew that his department was aware of the fact that he had taken a few days off. He had to come up with some reason to leave.

"I'll see you later," he replied. Then he left.

Thirty minutes later Cathy had made a choice. She would stay, just for a little while. It was then that another thought occurred to her, could she trust Mr. Derek Ryan not to tell anyone? She suddenly felt the need to follow him, but she knew that she could not because he had been gone for awhile now. Slowly she got out of bed, wrapped a sheet around her and walked to the window, opening it for some fresh air.

The day was beautiful as the sun shined brightly in the sky on an early summer day. Birds chirped happily from tree branches. One neighbor was mowing his lawn and cars occasionally drove by on the street, of which one was, she thought, a very pretty color. After a moment longer she went back to the bed and sat on its edge.

A child screamed and she jumped to her feet, being at the window in a moment's time. Her eyes quickly located the child and she breathed a sigh of relief. The child was only screaming at an older sibling who had snatched his toy. The older one pointed to the window with the intent to distract his little brother.

"See the kitty! Look at the kitty in the window. Isn't it a pretty kitty?"

The child ignored him, still wanting his toy. Realizing his ploy had not worked the boy turned and ran home, his little brother following closely behind, still screaming.

Cathy sat on the window sill, watching the world outside while her mind was in turmoil. She still had doubts about Derek. The fact that she had changed into a cat did make one thing clear, she was ready and able to leave. Her mind continued to dwell on these things as she watched a bird land on a neighboring tree. It sat there a moment, looking around, and then flew down the street to another tree where it succeeded in startling a squirrel. It chattered angrily at being interrupted and scampered along the branches to a nearby tree where it climbed down its trunk to the ground. The squirrel did not stay long before it scampered back from whence it had come after being startled, this time by a person sitting on a bench just below the tree.

Cathy was startled at first, then puzzled as she noticed that the person was Derek. He had told her he was going to the station. Why was he sitting under a tree? She suddenly decided to join him. She moved cautiously so as not to attract too much attention to herself. To others she just looked like a cat.

As she approached the bench Derek saw her which caused her to stop. Would he recognize her in her second form? They both stared at one another for a few moments, but to Cathy it felt like an eternity when Derek spoke.

"Well, hello cat. Nice kitty, kitty. Come to keep me company. I'm sorry that I can't stay though. After sitting here for awhile trying to sort through things I've suddenly decided to visit a good friend of mine. You're welcome to come if you like."

Cathy watched him get up and walk down the street and turn a corner. When he disappeared from her sight she took off after him. Derek walked two blocks then turned down a street. Half way down he turned onto a sidewalk leading up to a one-story house set back from the street. She watched him walk up a couple of steps and knock on the door. A moment passed in silence, then two. Cathy used that time to move closer as the door opened on the third moment. A woman stood in the frame-work of the structure, beautiful, slender, and agile. She wore a pair of blue jeans and a soft blue colored shirt, light blue socks and tennis shoes. Her face was in shadow. Upon catching sight of her visitor she released an excited shout of joy and jumped into his arms, giving him a huge hug.

"Derek, it's so good to see you. You hardly ever stop by. I've missed you."

"Ha-ha Celeste. Very funny, it's only been a couple of days."

"Way too many days. Come in, come in. I've just made a fresh cup of coffee."

Derek entered and as the door closed behind him Cathy zipped through unnoticed.

"As well as being so athletic now you're turning into a comedian on me?" Derek laughed softly as he sat on a rose covered love seat. It went well with the décor of the rest of the room. The walls were painted soft lavender. The carpet was a cream color, plush and soft under his feet. A beautiful landscape picture lined the wall above his head, reflecting a few other similar ones on the other walls. Some soft cushioned oak chairs and a baby grand piano helped to decorate the room.

Celeste laughed lightly as she sauntered into the kitchen to return moments later with two steaming mugs of the brew. She handed him one of the cups then settled herself in one of the oak chairs.

"I was just going to change my clothes to go jogging. Would you care to join me?"

Derek took a careful sip of the hot liquid before replying. "Thanks. I think I will pass today. I should really get down to the station soon, even thought I took some days off I need to check on a few things."

Cathy cringed inwardly at Celeste's words then shook herself for being so silly. All she had to do was to prove to her that she could trust this man. It mattered not if he had a girlfriend. Then how come her heart was telling her differently? She had only just met the man, for Christ's sake. She shook herself and sat down beside the love seat to listen; making sure Celeste could not see her.

"Now I know there is something wrong. You have never refused an invitation before. What's bothering you?"

"You could say a number of things." How could he tell her about Cathy without revealing her secret? He decided on a different subject, another puzzle that was so extreme he had no idea how to proceed, which was finding this creature, and stopping it before it could kill again. But there was one thing he did know; the town was not safe at night for it was clearly obvious the creature was a night hunter.

Celeste waited patiently. She knew Derek would elaborate further when he was ready. She smiled to herself, remembering their childhood as they grew up together. They had been very close throughout the years and it was still the same today.

"The main one is that creature. I saw him Celeste, two nights ago."

For a moment Celeste was speechless. "What are you going to do?"

"It has to be stopped."

"And how do you propose to do that? So far, the police have not been able to track it to find its hiding place. It like disappears."

"There has got to be a way to find it." Staring out the living room window, his brow furrowed, seeing a yellow tom cat walk among the bushes.

"There may be a way to do it. I need to check on something." Rising from his chair he started toward the door. Celeste followed. Turning to her he said, "Thank you for the coffee and the wonderful advice." With that he gave her a quick kiss on the cheek and left. Celeste stood in the open door for a moment, puzzled. Smiling she shook her head and closed the door, not seeing Cathy as she slipped through.

Sitting on the sidewalk she contemplated her next move. She knew the creature had to be killed and Derek would need help. With that Cathy moved toward home to plan.

Later that night, as Cathy walked through the park she noticed quite a few people out after the curfew. This was not good. The creature could show at any moment. These people needed to be indoors. Cathy found a seat near the base of a huge tree and sat down to wait. Hopefully she could warn them in time.

An hour passed with almost all of the people gone.

Cathy didn't pay much attention to the fact that she had changed again and quickly climbed the huge tree. She did wonder though, why the housecat and not the panther. She stretched out on a high branch and continued to wait.

By the time nine pm approached the sun had gone down hours ago. The park was now quiet so she moved to the fork of the tree to rest awhile. A few minutes passed when she heard a noise. Raising her head to look she saw a woman jogging. Cathy recognized her immediately, Derek's girlfriend. What was her name? Celeste! Why was she jogging so late?

To mingle with the recognition was the feeling of imminent danger. When Celeste reached the base of the tree Cathy let out a yowl. Celeste stopped and looked up.

"Hi cat. What's the matter? Are you stuck?"

Cathy moved back and forth trying to look confused. It worked. "Okay, I'll come up to help you" Celeste began to climb. When she reached the limb, the cat was on she felt something brush her right leg. She jumped, instinctively moving the leg faster as she sat on the branch and looked down. Her leg was bleeding from a long gash. She frowned and looked to the ground for some kind of explanation. What she saw made her sit so still that she reflected a statue, her eyes staring in wide wonder and fear. She knew what she was looking at from the description Derek had given her, but never in her wildest dreams did she ever think she would be this close to it.

The creature snarled, and then lunged at her, trying to knock her down. Celeste realized he could not climb, but even so she felt more distance between them was a good thing and climbed up to another branch. She noted the cat did not follow her. Instead, it sat on the branch as though teasing the creature, growling and hissing.

Celeste realized the cat had inadvertently saved her life, or deliberately, she wasn't sure. Did the cat know the creature was close by?

"Here…kitty…kitty," slurred the creature.

Celeste jumped when she heard the animal speak.

"Come down and…play."

The cat stood her ground, tail moving in agitation, rapidly back and forth. She had no intention of coming down and the creature knew it.

The creature's eyes narrowed, watching his intended prey. There was something different about this cat and he wanted to find out what it was. He circled the tree, testing it for a way up while Cathy watched his every move.

Facing the cat again the creature spoke, "There is something different with…you. I sense…it."

Cathy growled low, ears bent back, tail swishing rapidly.

"You act tough, but there is fear I feel as…well."

"Leave now! You are not wanted."

Celeste's eyes grew round as she looked at the cat. Did she just hear it talk?

"I was…right. You are like…me."

"No, maybe in speech, but I am no killer."

"Even so I will know all about you before I kill…you!" With that he crouched low and propelled himself up.

Derek was furious after going home to find Cathy gone. Even though it was getting late he went over to his sisters to find her gone as well. This was not good. There was a curfew in effect and his sister was most likely jogging. Even he was taking a chance. Sitting in his car he decided to follow a route he knew his sister would take. What he found totally floored him as the beams from his headlights caught the scene. He saw the creature leap to a nearby branch, missing it as a house cat leaped at it, landing on top of its head. Digging the claws in deep, scratching and biting caused the creature to release the branch and fall to the ground, roaring out in pain and anger.

As he landed the cat was off and running. Turning to give chase the creature noticed the headlights for the first time and saw the movement of a man aim a weapon at him. He roared as blood dripped into his eye and turned to flee, wincing as one of the bullets hit his leg.

Derek raced to the foot of the tree, aiming the gun at the empty space the animal had disappeared firing off two more shots before he realized there was nothing there. Looking up into the tree he saw Celeste, eyes wide and tear filled. Helping her down Celeste clung to him. Wiping away her tears he said, "Come, let's get you home."

Sitting in the bushes the yellow tom cat watched and learned. He turned and left then, knowing what he needed to do.

Six

After returning from the hospital with stitches in the gash on her leg and a crutch Celeste gave Derek some bedding for the couch and went to bed, Derek left the house and entered his patrol car to use the in-car computer used to research police databases. He needed to check on Miss Cathy Ryler, especially after what Celeste had told him. Two shapes, she could change into two distinct animals. After logging into the precincts system, he ran some checks through and found nothing. The same came from his contacts with the FBI. Her address was listed. She had a sister living in Princeton, Minnesota. Otherwise, she lived alone, a single woman after the death of her husband. Starting another search, he hit on something. Reading the police report he saw that she was attacked by someone while visiting her sister. It said that she could not remember even being attacked due to a head injury. There was the key. He felt it. He needed to talk to her, right away.

Clayton Cartel looked in the mirror at the cut above his left eye; so much for his good looks. It would definitely leave a scar. Sitting on a chair in his apartment he examined the wound below his right knee. He was fortunate the bullet only grazed him. Placing a bandage over it he thought of his plans for tonight, when his anger would seek the revenge, he needed. Now he needed to find two animals. They were a threat to his survival. He also needed to find the Riley woman, one of three enemies he needed to kill. She was the main one, the one responsible for his problems. So far, he has not seen her return to her home, although he had missed a couple of times. As for that police officer, he would be a sideline treat to end his quest since he could find him easily. Right now he was very tired and needed sleep.

Come night fall the creature walked between two houses, listening while smelling the air for any signs of prey. He saw a dog on the other side of the street. Crouching low he prepared to spring the distance and take the animal. He stared at his victim, gauging the distance he would need. Suddenly the sound of loose rock being kicked reached his ears causing him to stop his hunt. He looked to see what it was. The dog was immediately forgotten when he saw a woman walking in his direction. He crouched low and waited.

Cathy was enjoying her walk until a few minutes ago. Something did not feel right. She felt that someone was watching her and something else that she did not usually feel…fear. It increased the more steps she took. She quickened the pace, deciding to cross the street. Suddenly she stopped, smelling something in the air. Before she could identify it, she heard the squeal of tires and looked up to see headlights bearing down on her. Before she thought twice, she leapt straight into the air, quickly noting the car as it passed below her and watched it, as she landed, loose control and run head long into a pole. The impact caused both doors to open, the driver falling to the ground. Without thinking she ran to the car to check on the driver. Satisfied that he was all right for the time being she went to the other side and helped the other man out.

He sat against the car, closing his eyes for a moment while Cathy checked the cut on his forehead. It was obvious both needed medical attention. As she worked, she suddenly felt the boy tense. She looked at his face, fearing he was having some kind of attack, noting his eyes were open. He was staring straight ahead, his eyes growing larger. His hands pushed his back up against the car as though he was trying to get away by climbing up its side. It was then that Cathy felt something or someone behind her.

The creature sat in the shadows for a few minutes after the scene with the car. No one, not anybody could jump straight into the air and higher than a car. It wasn't possible. Only cats could jump like that. He had to find out more from her before he killed them.

When Cathy turned around to face what was behind her, her feet froze and would not move. There before her stood the source of her nightmare, more chilling and deadly than in her dreams.

He was covered from head to tail in brown fur darkened in spots. Her stomach recoiled when she realized the spots were patches of dried blood. His teeth were long, some extending below the others and stained red. Powerful muscles rippled under his fur as he slowly moved toward her. His claws were longer than her fingers.

She jumped at the start of a voice, realizing the creature had spoken.

"How…did…you…do…that?"

The creature waited for an answer, impatient. His short tail switched in agitation as he took a step forward.

Cathy was in a dilemma. The young man beside her had painfully crawled back into the car, as well as the driver, locking them inside. She could not change, but she knew she would. There was no way of getting out of it.

"Do what?"

"Jump…straight…in…the…air. Tell…me…before…I…kill."

The creature took another step foreword and that was the last straw. Cathy changed. Not into a house cat, but into a huge, black leopard. Before the creature could register what happened Cathy attacked. Before she could think twice, she went for his throat. Seeing her coming at him he swatted her to the side, and then pounced on top of her. She snarled up at him.

"I know who you are-now. You were in the park when I tried to catch a yellow cat. My three to find is now two. Although I wonder, could you also be the cat in the tree a few days ago with a woman? You caused me pain and ruined my life, now you will-die."

Cathy felt the claws dig into her shoulder. She cried out, retaliating by bringing her back legs up to slice at his belly. The creature cried out, releasing her. Cathy scrambled away and ran, disappearing into the night. The creature recovered enough to see her leave. He did not follow. He needed to tend his wounds. He was fortunate she missed his internal organs, although it was close. Forgetting the two guys in the car he left. He would find her again, very soon.

As the sun began to brighten the sky Derek walked up the short flight of steps, down a short hall and faced the door to Cathy's apartment, a two-story duplex containing two apartments. Knocking once he waited for a response, and again when none came. He jumped when his long-range walkie-talkie beeped. Unclipping it from his belt he pressed the key to respond.

"Sergeant Ryan here."

"Dispatch here. Sergeant, we need you at Blakely Street ASAP. There has been another attack."

Derek swore under his breath. "I'm on my way."

"And Sergeant, there are survivors."

Entering the street Derek was greeted with flashing red and blue lights of parked squad cars blocking any oncoming traffic and keeping the media at bay; and one parked ambulance.

After verifying his credentials with the officer guarding the perimeter Derek approached the scene. Seeing one of the victims was being wheeled on a gurney into the ambulance he stopped the paramedic for a moment. He moved back a bit to let the Sergeant talk.

Derek looked at the young man, a boy of fourteen; seeing the cut on his forehead. When the boy opened his eyes and saw Derek he said, "You have to help her. She saved us from that creature. He hurt her."

"I will son. I'll find her."

Derek moved back a bit to let the paramedics put him into the ambulance. As he moved the next words from him chilled Derek. "She changed. I saw her change." The paramedics shook their heads, thinking he was being delusional as they closed the door and left.

Moving to where one of the officers stood, a young man in his early thirties, Derek asked for details on what happened. His ID said his name was Kincaid and he was all too happy to enlighten Derek.

"It seems the father swerved to miss hitting a woman who was standing in the road, which resulted from them hitting the pole. From that it gets a bit strange. The woman checked them both for injuries, and when tending to the boy the confrontation happened. The boy witnessed it. Said a huge creature, like a deformed Saber Tooth tiger came up behind them. The woman turned to confront him and…this was the best part…she transformed, shape shifted into a black panther and they fought."

"Your right officer Kincaid, that is strange. The kid must have bumped his head more than we thought."

Kincaid nodded agreement and left. Derek began to walk the perimeter, looking for the tell-tale signs of a struggle. No one noticed him, each one busy with his or her tasks. Moving over the area Derek soon found the results of a struggle. Broken and smashed blades of grass, weeds pressed into the ground and dirt pushed up. Mixed in were two distinct paw prints. Searching further he saw the direction each went; relieved the creature had not given chase.

Following Cathy's prints, he saw they disappeared in some bushes. Did she change back? How hurt was she? Leaving the scene in the capable hands of his officers he decided to go back to Cathy's apartment.

Cathy rested on the couch. The wound in her shoulder was just about healed. The bruises would take a bit longer. Her ability to change into a house cat was awe inspiring and unreal, but to change into two distinct animals was totally bizarre. She was still trying to absorb it all. Closing her eyes she began to drift off. At the sound of a loud knock on her door, followed closely by another she sat bolt upright. When she heard Derek's voice she relaxed.

"Cathy, Cathy are you in there?! Cathy!"

"The door is open. You can come in."

Cathy watched him closely as Derek walked into the living room. Dressed in his black uniform and policeman's belt encircling his midriff he presented a striking image. When she saw the expression on his face, she curbed the feeling that coursed through her system as she watched him walk toward her. Moving slightly, she winced and he was immediately by her side, eyes wide, concern evident on his face.

"You have been hurt. You need to lay back and rest."

She smiled weakly up at him. Pulling a chair over he sat in front of her.

"We need to talk Cathy. I believe this all started from the accident you had while visiting your sister. Can you remember anything more about it?

"I remember being knocked down. Then struggling to breathe, fighting the weight holding me down and a sudden sharp pain in my right hip. I also saw a flash of a syringe as I fell. I don't know why I remembered it. It happened so fast."

"You did not see the man?"

"No, to me his face was all in black."

"He most likely wore a face mask."

"I did remember one thing about him. He has a mark of some kind on his neck, like maybe a birthmark. In the struggle I must have moved the mask, but did not connect it till later, when my head cleared.

"Ya, the report mentioned you hurt your head."

"I also found some strange papers in my purse when I returned home. I kept one and threw the others away. The man found the ones in the waste basket and took a copy of the one I kept. It was the same man who knocked me down because I saw the mark."

Derek blinked. "Whoa whoa, back up here. What do you mean he took it?"

"He broke into my place a few days back. I had played around with the original copy because I was fascinated with the symbols. He found the copy and took it."

Shocked Derek said, "You had a break-in and never reported it?!"

She shrugged her shoulders. "I never got the chance."

He shook his head. "Where is the original copy?"

"In my bedroom, top dresser door, inside a small loose board on the left side of the drawer."

Derek rose, entered the room and quickly found the paper. Donning gloves he looked it over as he returned to the chair.

Cathy asked, "Do you know what it is?"

"It looks like some type of formula equation. I will take it to our lab; have it checked out." Retrieving a plastic bag from his pocket he inserted the paper, folded it and placed it inside his shirt pocket.

"What happened last night? Why did you fight that creature again?"

"I didn't have much choice. He came up behind us."

"The young boy said he saw you change?"

"Yes, I could not stop it. I did not want to, but when the creature took a step toward me, it happened. He said something strange when he had me pinned. He said he knew who I was. How could he know that?"

A chill passed through Derek at her words. "He talked, like you?"

"Yes. That surprised me too. The first time was in the park."

"This is not good. We need to leave here, now!"

He helped her to her feet. Derek wasn't sure why, but he cared for this woman more than he wanted to admit.

"You feel up to getting a few things together quick?"

"Yes." Limping to her bedroom she stopped in the doorway, turned to face him.

"I don't think he will show soon. He was hurt too. I hurt him good." With that she turned and entered her room, leaving Derek staring after her as he stood in the middle of the living room.

A while later Cathy sat in Derek's police car waiting while Derek dropped off the paper. She watched the people walking the streets in the late afternoon. A couple strode together across the street, walking hand-in-hand. A chubby store owner stepped out for some fresh air, greeting the couple as they passed. A boy zipped down her side of the street on a skateboard, nearly running into a woman as she walked her dog. As the lady walked past some bushes in front of the police station the dog suddenly pulled on the leash, barking hysterically at an invisible presence hidden inside the bushes. Scolding her dog the lady pulled him back and they proceeded down the street.

A moment passed, then two and Cathy jumped when the yellow tom cat landed onto the hood of the car. Smiling she opened the car door allowing the cat to have access to her lap, which he quickly took advantage of. Petting him as he purred softly, she said, "I guess you are thanking me for saving your tail the other night. Well, you are very welcome."

At that moment the other car door opened and Derek climbed into the driver's seat. Seeing the cat he said, "I have seen him before. He gets around a lot."

Cathy grinned, "I can imagine."

He glanced sideways at her as he started the car, and then rolled his eyes as he caught the double meaning to her words. When the engine rolled over the cat decided to leave. Pushing against Cathy in one last cat hug he exited the car. Cathy watched him as he disappeared around the building. Closing her car door they drove off.

"I am going to take you to Celeste's. Even though you met her briefly she is a great person and I know you will like her. Also, thank you for saving her life. She is so special to me."

Cathy stiffened at the sound of the name and her heart sank at his words.

"Are you sure she won't mind." Weakly hoping he would change his line of thinking. When he pulled into her driveway, she knew she lost the battle. Following him along the small sidewalk and up to the front door she stood beside him as he knocked. When the door opened the woman who stood on the threshold was able to take a man's breath away, exceeding natural beauty and extreme grace. She didn't stand a chance.

"Hi sis!"

Cathy looked puzzled. What did he just say? Did she hear him correctly?

Smiling Celeste said, "So who have you brought this time?"

Turning toward Cathy, Derek said, "Cathy, this is my sister Celeste. Celeste, this is Cathy Ryler."

"It's nice to meet you, Cathy."

For a moment Cathy was stunned to silence. "It's…it's nice to meet you too."

Celeste led them into a mid-sized kitchen, containing a refrigerator, cooking/prep space, a sink and a dishwasher on one side. A kitchen island was in the center with stools spaced around it. Beyond that was the dining area, combining the whole unit into a common, very functional room. Walking to the stove she poured a cup of coffee and held it out to Cathy.

"Would you like a cup of coffee?"

Accepting the cup Cathy sat on one of the stools.

"Derek?"

"No thanks. I need to get back to the station. Is it alright for Cathy to spend some time with you? I don't want her to be alone right now."

"Of course, that will be fine."

"You're a sweet one. Thank you much." Planting a quick thank you kiss on her cheek he left them. Walking to his car Derek got behind the wheel fighting his emotions. When he first realized how much in danger, she was in he wanted to grab her and drag her from the apartment. As he drove, he thought of the creature as well, the animal could speak, which meant he had a human form. That was the reason they could not find him. He was right under their noses.

Once at the station he went to his office. He could see a few of the other officers in the department working at their stations or coming in for a shift change. Setting to work on trying to locate the creature he was startled at the sudden knock on his door. He looked up to see a man standing there looking rather haggard.

"Can I help you?"

"Sorry for interrupting you. Your receptionist said I could come back to talk to one of you. My name is Clayton Cartel and I was hoping you could help me with a problem. I need to file a missing person's report."

"Ok, the person you need to help with that is the Records Clerk. He can help you with filling out the needed paperwork. His office is just inside the door as you come in."

Clayton's eyes narrowed slightly. This was the man he wanted to kill, the man who shot him. He would love to right now, but could not. There would be another time, very soon. It was a promise he intended to keep. "Thank you, sergeant, I did not know the right department to go to." With that he turned and left.

With the interruption Derek decided to get something to eat and go home. Once there he made the choice to get some sleep even though it was six thirty pm. By seven he was asleep. At two am he was jerked awake by his land line phone. Holding the receiver to his ear he said, "Ryan here."

"Sergeant, this is officer Kincaid. I am afraid the creature has struck again. We are on Butler Street."

Ok, I will be right there."

Jumping out of bed he did a quick half bath, wishing he could jump in the shower, dressed and was out the door in less than fifteen minutes. Arriving on the scene he was greeted by the typical barriers that separated the crime scene from the public. Passing through he met with several officers to get a run down of what happened from their perspective. From there he walked over to what was left of the body to talk to the medical examiner.

"What you got for me Blake?"

Bending over the body Blake shook his head. "There is nothing I haven't seen before, except now."

"What's that?"

"It's the same killer all right, but now he is leaving messages."

Derek's puzzled expression was enough. Blake moved aside. Looking at the body as it lay in a disheveled heap Derek saw what Blake referred to. Beside the body, written in the sand were the words, 'Found you.'

A chill passed through Derek. Turning to the crime analyst and anyone else who would hear him he said, "Make sure to take detailed pictures of everything and detailed documentation." Not noticing the flash of cameras Derek moved back, racing to his car and had dispatch put a call through to his sister. Groggily Celeste soon answered.

"Celeste, are you both doing, ok?"

"Derek…we are fine. Do you know what time it is?"

Yes, and I am sorry. Go back to sleep. I'll see you later."

Hanging up he leaned back against the seat and breathed a sigh of relief. Exiting the car, he caught movement in his peripheral vision from across the street, between two houses. There was something there. Walking toward it he drew his gun. Halfway there he felt something brush heavily against his legs. Looking down he saw the yellow tom cat weaving back-and-forth, not letting him take a step forward, and literally blocking his path.

"Cat, you need to move."

"Sergeant Ryan!"

Looking over his shoulder Derek saw officer Kincaid.

"We need you over here sir."

Looking toward his intended target Derek shook his head, turned around and walked back to the crime scene. The yellow tom stood there, gazing into the darkness shading the houses, not covered by the street lights.

"Come here cat," the creature hissed, not happy he was cheated out of another sweet anticipated kill.

The cat hissed and ran in the opposite direction. The creature let out a huge roar in frustration and anger at the cat, the sound echoing off houses and trees. Everyone at the crime scene stopped what they were doing. Derek quickly rounded up several officers to search, but to no avail. The animal was gone.

Hours later, as the sun began to climb up from the horizon Derek walked into the station to work on the paper work side of the case and assess the next move. Sitting down at his computer he began to type. Ten minutes into the mix his phone rings.

"This is Sergeant Ryan."

"Hello, Sergeant Ryan. This is Sam Benson, a tech from the forensic lab. I have the results of the paper you dropped off here."

"Go ahead. I'm listening."

"It consists of a chemical equation to apply a process that changes shapes and forms into something else. I was able to recover two sets of prints. One belongs to a Cathy Ryler, who lives here in town. The other is a Professor Matthews. He lived in Princeton, Minnesota."

"Lived?"

"Yes, it seems he was murdered a few months back. He worked at a research facility in that town."

"Thank you, Benson."

After hanging up Derek quickly finished what he was doing and left. He knew what he needed to do now. First, he needed to check in on Cathy. Approaching his sister's home, he knocked gently on the door and was met with a scowling, arms crossed sister. Wincing he knew he was in for a chew out session or the silent treatment.

"I said I was sorry sis."

She gave a small snort of disapproval and turned back into the house. Following her Derek went into the living room where Cathy sat holding the yellow tom cat. Leaving them Celeste went to the kitchen.

Derek said, "I see you have made a friend there."

Cathy smiled, "And he seems to have made a few of his own too. There were several outside. Did you see them?"

"No."

"I am not surprised. They probably hid when they saw you coming. I can assure you, they are close by, watching."

For some reason Derek believed her.

"I wanted to see how you were doing and to let you know I will be leaving town, hopefully to be home by tonight."

"Does it have to do with the creature?"

"I hope to have all the answers to catch him."

Placing the cat on the floor she said, "Good. Let me walk you out." Stopping on the front step Cathy watched him walk away. "Be safe."

Derek stopped, turned around and walked up to Cathy taking note of her, newly cut, short blond hair, almond shaped eyes, heart shaped face and the soft full lips. Placing his hand gently on the back of her head he brought his lips to meet hers. The kiss was tender and sweet, leaving Cathy breathless for more when Derek broke free and left. Derek knew if he did not leave now, he would not be leaving at all. Once on the road he had lots of time to think.

Seven

Still wrestling with his emotions Derek found himself standing in front of the Microbiology Research building in Princeton, located in the West End area of St. Louis Park. The facility dealt mostly in large animal research with animal care, veterinary knowledge, and maintenance of housing facilities for animal-related research activities.

Entering the building he approached a receptionist, a young woman in her twenties offering a bright smile in greeting and a willingness to assist. He showed her his credentials and asked who would be the best person to talk to regarding the murders he was investigating.

"That would be Professor Billings. Let me page him for you."

Derek thanked her and waited. Soon a man in his late fifties walked toward him, holding out his hand and smiling, showing even white teeth. He looked the typical professor with his glasses on his forehead, a cheerful face and receding hair line. Derek reached out to meet the man and shook his hand.

"Thank you for meeting with me Professor Billings. I am investigating several murders in my town and would like to ask you some questions."

"No problem. I would be happy to help any way I can. Let's go to my office where we can talk." Once in his office they settled in, Professor Billings behind his desk and Derek in a chair facing him.

"This involves a man who was killed here, a Dr. Matthews? Do you have any idea what he had been working on before he was killed?"

"Yes, such a sad thing to have happened. He was quite secretive about his project, but it was rumored he was working on a way to shape shift someone; an interesting concept by far, but not likely to happen, especially now that he has died. The police discovered some of his papers. A notebook, one missing test tube and a filled syringe were the only items taken. Soon after that it was discovered an employee had not shown up and no one can find him. It is thought that he was responsible for killing the good doctor."

"May I ask his name? He may be one I need to talk to."

"Yes. His name is Clayton Cartel."

Derek blinked as the name registered, almost totally missing the professors next words.

"There have also been some nasty murders here in town. Most of them are prostitutes and the police are quite baffled because it is some kind of animal tearing people to pieces. The town has a curfew since they seem to happen at night. I don't think they would call that a serial killer because that usually refers to a person, don't you think?"

"Yes, I believe so. Thank you, Professor Billings. You have been a big help." Shaking the man's hand Derek left, almost bumping into a man standing outside the door. The man's eyes narrowed as he watched Derek leave the building.

Driving back home Derek could not believe what he had found out. It was obvious Cathy had been injected with the serum from the stolen syringe and so was Mr. Cartel, not to mention Cartel had been standing in the doorway of his office, not but a few hours ago. Getting on his car radio he called the station to put an all points bulletin for Clayton Cartel. After the call he remembered the other bomb shell Professor Billings mentioned. Was Clayton traveling back and forth? What was his connection to the town besides working there? After dwelling on these questions and others he finally made it back to Manchester.

Deciding to go to the station first before seeing Cathy he pulled into the driveway. Seeing that someone had parked a van in his reserved spot he parked opposite it. Walking between it and another car he took note of the license plate. As he passed the side door it opened and Derek suddenly found himself on the ground. Hands began picking him up and putting him into the van, his hands and feet bound tightly and tape placed across his mouth. Everything happened so fast he had no time to react. As the door closed and the van backed up, he began to kick feverishly, struggling to try and get free. This resulted in the van pulling over and the driver move to the back and placing a chloroformed cloth over Derek's nose. Derek quickly stopped struggling and lay still.

"Can't have you making a lot of noise Sergeant Ryan; plus, I don't need you so bruised up because I plan on you bringing Cathy out of hiding." Clayton returned to the driver's seat and pulled away from the curb. Traveling a few miles out of town he entered a huge construction site. Driving up to an abandoned warehouse he carried the man inside, oblivious to watching eyes.

Officer Kincaid and two other officers exited the police station in time to see the van leave the parking lot. Right away they noticed the sergeant's car parked in the wrong slot. Walking over to it they noted the engine was still warm.

Kincaid said, "Did you two see the Sergeant in the building?"

Officer Jacob Simmons said, "His office was dark when I walked past it."

The other officer, Lance Williams agreed with Jacob. He had not seen the sergeant any where inside. Knowing the man would be in his office when here after hours they realized something was wrong. When it became obvious, he could not be located anywhere they called his sister to see if she had heard from him.

When Celeste answered the phone, they had just finished eating a late supper. Listening intently and answering the needed questions she hung up the phone. The worried expression on her face warned Cathy that something was wrong.

Looking at Cathy, Celeste said, "I guess Derek stopped at the station to see to the progress on a man hunt he started while driving back to town and they cannot find him. It's as though he just disappeared. They fear he may have been kidnapped, but have no idea by whom."

"Did the officer say who they were hunting?"

"No, only that he is wanted for questioning concerning a number of murders and is the prime suspect."

Cathy did not like this. Something inside her said Derek wasn't just kidnapped, but in serious mortal danger. She had to find him.

"Celeste, I need to go look for him."

"No, you can't. It is almost dark!"

"I will be all right."

They both jumped at the loud sound of a cat yowling. Both women went to the front door. Stepping outside they saw the yellow tom cat with another smaller cat. The smaller one looked at Cathy and yowled again. Cathy knew what she had to do as she watched the cat run down the sidewalk to its end and stop to look at her again. There was danger, Cathy could feel it now.

"I think that cat wants you to follow it."

"She does. Promise me you will stay here."

Celeste hesitated. Cathy lifted her chin, giving her a direct look. "Alright, I promise."

Cathy nodded her head. Walking off the small porch and up to where the cat waited, she nodded once and they took off. As they ran Cathy changed.

Derek moaned as he began to wake up. His wrists and ankles ached from the restraints. When he opened his eyes, he took in his surroundings. He was in a very large room with sky-walks running along the outer edge. Below them, placed periodically were doors leading away from the room, some rusted open. Several boxes and crates sat empty and discarded against the walls. He sat on a chair, directly in the center of the room, bound tightly.

"I see you are finally awake."

Derek now focused on the man standing directly in front of him. He knew he was looking at Clayton Cartel. His eyes narrowed as he struggled against his restraints.

"There, there now. All is not lost Sergeant. We just have to finish where we left off the other day. It was about a missing person. Oh no! Where are my manners? You can't tell me with your mouth covered." With a quick flash of his hand, he ripped the tape from Derek's mouth.

"You murdering son-of-b---"

"Now, now Sergeant, such language coming from a man of the law, all I want is the location of the Ryler woman. I know she is hiding somewhere because I have been keeping an eye on her apartment. She hasn't been home lately."

"Sorry, I am not in the mood to help you. I don't make it a habit of helping sadistic killers."

The sudden whack as Clayton's hand connected with Derek's jaw sent his head reeling. Derek looked up at Clayton, tasting blood from his cut lip. Clayton hit him again, resulting in daggers coming from Derek's eyes.

"I will ask one more time. Where is she?!"

"Right behind you."

Clayton turned at the sound of Cathy's voice to see a sleek black leopard walking toward him. He smiled.

"Well now, it's so nice to see you. Interesting, I don't sense much if any fear from you. What has changed? No matter. You will die just the same."

Crouching low, ready to spring Cathy did have some fear, but it did not overwhelm her as before. Now she had a purpose; to save the man she loved.

"Leave her alone you sick bastard."

Turning back to Derek Clayton said, "There you go with the swearing again. Well, I don't think I need you any more, Sergeant. I am going to enjoy this."

As Derek watched, the man's shape changed. The ferocious beast that faced him now sent chills through him. Derek's eyes grew wide at the sudden appearance of Cathy poised above him as she jumped onto the creature's back. Her claws dug deep into his side and her teeth clamped tight onto the back of his neck.

The creature reared up roaring in pain and anger. Immediately he tried to dislodge her by rolling to his side, and then onto his back. It worked as Cathy could not take the full weight of him, quickly releasing him. The creature jumped to his feet, turning to face his opponent. Cathy did the same. No fear. This was the panther now, fierce, lethal, knowing this was the final confrontation. Ears back against her head she roared.

Derek pulled hard against his restraints trying in vain to get free when he felt something touch his wrist. He quickly looked at the source and saw his sister.

"Celeste, what are you doing here?"

Continuing to untie him she said, "I know I promised Cathy, but I saw one of the cats go past the house and decided to follow it."

"One of the cats?"

It was that moment Derek noticed cats all around them, surrounding the creature. Each one began to attack in a sporadic pattern while jumping onto the creatures back, sinking their claws deep, and some hitting the already open wounds. The creature tried to reach the cats, but they quickly moved out of his reach. When the animals on his back dug in deep with claws and teeth, he arched up to dislodge them. The distraction was what the panther desired, giving her the opening she needed, straight shot to the throat. Sinking her teeth in deep, clasping her jaws tight in the strangle hold she used the force of her weight to bring him down. That, combined with the cats tearing his back to shreds and loss of blood he began to weaken. When he laid still the cats left, but the panther stayed her ground, holding…holding.

Minutes passed. With no movement the panther released her hold and walked over to Derek, the cats and Celeste.

"I thought you promised not to follow, Celeste."

Celeste looked at the panther and said, "Cathy! How, what happened? When I saw that man change into the creature I about fell over."

Derek said, "We can explain it later. We should leave. I need to call this in."

Celeste looked at Derek. "You mean you knew of this?"

Derek winced and said, "I knew about Cathy but not the identity of the creature until I went to Princeton. We can discuss this later Celeste."

They jumped when one of the cats hissed, and then another. Turning they looked at the creature. He had not moved, but beside him now stood a man, five and a half feet tall he stood at his full height. Well-dressed, middle-aged he spoke volumes due to the authority he presented. Looking at the creature, still lifeless he said, "Serves you right for killing my butler. I can't figure it out. How can you talk when changed and I can't. A memory flashed before him as he walked into his home after spending several overnight stays at his lab across town to see everything disheveled. Things were busted, furniture broken and scattered around, pictures torn from the walls and smashed on the floor. At the end of it all was finding the mutilated body of his butler and friend, Simon. That, combined with the scent of blood activated an intense rage within him. For the first time since injecting himself with the formula he felt himself change, his limbs transform. With that memory he looked at the group focusing on the panther, which was the source of all his problems.

Cathy roared loudly, crouching low; the entire cat's growled and hissed again, arching their backs high. Derek is puzzled until he sees the man change in front of them, his clothes landing at his feet. When done a beast stood in front of them. He snarled and charged at them. The cats split up to circle him as the panther met him head on. Derek pushed his sister out of the way as he drew his gun. Aiming it point blank he fired. The beast jerked back from the bullets as the cats jumped on the beast's back. He was larger than the creature, his skin thicker, which made the cats work harder. When the panther hit him with the full force of her body, he was knocked off his feet. Once down the panther quickly grabbed the beast at the side of his neck, holding on.

The beast felt himself weakening due to the bullets, but he still tried to jerk free. The cats were not helping either. Finally, he got what he wanted as the cats quickly left him and the panther released him.

He wasn't sure why, but quickly rose to his feet, swinging around to see what he could catch of them and found himself facing a new, but old enemy. Standing in front of him was the creature, blood dripping from his neck wound and back he had gained enough strength from his unconscious state to wake up. Now he faced the beast, Fabian his old enemy. The two animals clashed, tearing and ripping at each other. The others moved back and watched. Outside a storm moved in bringing loud claps of thunder and splitting shafts of lightening. All that went unnoticed as the cats left and the three continued to watch, waiting to see who survived. They jumped when a shaft of lightening struck the building. Soon smoke entered the room followed by bits of flame, quickly spreading throughout the building.

Derek yelled, "We need to get out of here. If I remember this old warehouse have containers of gasoline and other explosives in the other rooms. He no more than spoke when one of the rooms exploded. All three took off, leaving the combatants behind. Once outside and safely away they looked back in time to see more explosions and the building burn.

Cathy lay down on the grass and changed back to her human form.

Derek said, "Celeste can you go find the van I came in? Hopefully before it rains"

A loud clap of thunder answered Derek's claim followed by a flash of lightening.

"I was able to bring my car. Once I saw the direction the cats were going, I came back to get the car. We use to play here as kids, remember? I will be right back."

Derek smiled and walked over to Cathy.

"I think I hurt my leg, Derek."

Bending down he helped her sit up and lean against a tree.

"We will take you to the doctor and have it checked out. I am so glad you are ok."

"So am I."

His lips touched hers in a soft kiss, tender at first, exploring. Cathy accepted the softness his lips gave, responding in kind. Pulling back reluctantly she looked into his eyes and said, "Take me home." Picking her up in his arms he kissed her again. Sighing she placed her arms around his neck and her head against his shoulder. He walked in the direction his sister had disappeared, ignoring the rain drops that began to fall.

Later that night, after the storm passed by the cat sat on top of the car watching a group of kids walk down the street. They had no idea they had a watcher of the night observing their movements.